This Walker book belongs to:

. . . .

. . . .

. . . .

For Karen, who cares
B. B.

To Frieda
K. M. D.

First published 2011 by Walker Books Ltd
87 Vauxhall Walk, London SE11 5HJ

This edition published 2012

2 4 6 8 10 9 7 5 3 1

Text © 2011 Bonny Becker
Illustrations © 2011 Kady MacDonald Denton

The right of Bonny Becker and Kady MacDonald Denton to be identified
as author and illustrator respectively of this work has been asserted by them
in accordance with the Copyright, Designs and Patents Act 1988

This book has been typeset in New Baskerville

Printed in China

All rights reserved. No part of this book may be reproduced, transmitted or
stored in an information retrieval system in any form or by any means,
graphic, electronic or mechanical, including photocopying, taping and
recording, without prior written permission from the publisher.

British Library Cataloguing in Publication Data:
a catalogue record for this book is available from the British Library

ISBN 978-1-4063-3856-0

www.walker.co.uk

The Sniffles for Bear

Bonny Becker

illustrated by
Kady MacDonald Denton

WALKER BOOKS
AND SUBSIDIARIES
LONDON • BOSTON • SYDNEY • AUCKLAND

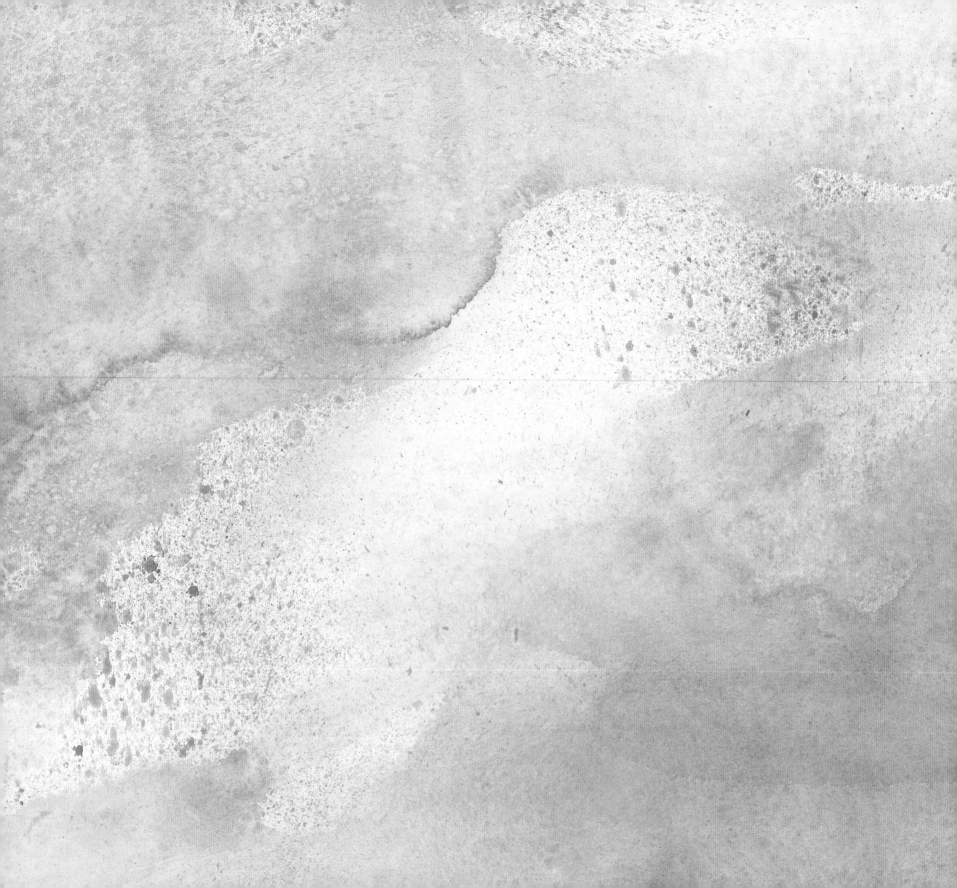

Bear was ill, very, very ill.

His eyes were red. His snout was red.

His throat was sore and gruffly.

In fact, Bear was quite sure no one

had ever been as ill as he was.

One morning, Bear heard a *tap, tap, tapping* on his front door.

"Cub in!" he rasped.

Mouse, small and grey and bright-eyed, bustled into Bear's living room.

Bear huddled in his chair. Big and brown and sniffly-snouted.

He had a terrible cold.

"I am come!" declared Mouse. "Soon you'll be as good as new!"

Bear frowned. Mouse was much too cheerful.

"I am quite ill," Bear reminded him.

"Indeed," said Mouse. "I have just the thing."

Mouse riffled through his bag, then settled next to Bear with a yellow book in his paw.

"'It was spring,'" Mouse read. "'The sky was blue. The sun was happy. All the birds were singing.'"

"Stop!" growled Bear. "I fear you do not appreciate the gravity of my situation."

Mouse looked sad, but his tail didn't.

"In fact, I may not be long for this world," Bear huffed.

"Oh, my," Mouse said.

"Yes," Bear murmured, coughing pitifully. "I grow weaker by the moment."

"Aah, I have just the thing," Mouse announced. "I shall soothe you with a song. *Oooooooh, she'll be coming round the mountain when she comes. She'll be coming round the mountain when she comes. She'll be coming—*"

"Disgraceful!" barked Bear.

"Don't you like singing?" asked Mouse.

"When someone is dreadfully ill, you sing mournful songs.

 Everyone knows that," growled Bear. He blew his nose with a honk.

"I have just the thing," Mouse said.

He riffled through his bag.

Plunk! Plink! Plunkety, twing, twang, plonk! Mouse strummed heartily
on a tiny banjo.

"That isn't mournful at all!" cried Bear.

"It gets sad later," Mouse promised. *Twing, twang, plunk—*

"This is impossible, intolerable—" Bear started to roar, but he was too weak.

"Look!" Bear wheezed. "Look at how my paw is trembling. You must help me to my bed."

And, indeed, Mouse was most helpful.

He tucked Bear in, then whisked out of
the bedroom door.

He returned balancing a big bowl
of soup on his head.

"Nettle soup," Mouse said.

"I made it myself."

Bear sipped cautiously. It was hot and tasted a bit like spinach and straw. Bear rather liked it. His eyes began to close.

"Better?" enquired Mouse.

Bear's eyes snapped open.

"Certainly not! I think I should make a will."

"Ahhhh, I have just the thing," said Mouse, fetching a pencil and
little notebook from his bag.
He perched next to Bear, his pencil poised to write.
Bear gazed thoughtfully at the ceiling. "I, Bear," he said,
"leave my red roller skates to…"

Bear paused. Mouse leaned forward eagerly.

"To Mouse," announced Bear.

"Hooray!" said Mouse.

Bear frowned. "You needn't be so happy about it.

I also leave my mop to Mouse," he added quickly.

Mouse didn't look so interested in that.

"And my wash bucket," added Bear.

At last, Mouse seemed to understand the gravity of the situation.

"Anything else?" asked Mouse.

"I'm too weak to go on," said Bear.

"Perhaps I could just add your kettle," said Mouse helpfully.

"HAVE YOU NO DECENCY?"

bellowed Bear, sitting bolt upright in bed.

"Your strength has returned!" Mouse exclaimed.

"No, it hasn't," said Bear, falling back. "That was just the last

flicker before the dark."

"I see." Mouse folded his paws and looked very sad …

even his tail.

Bear's voice dropped to a whisper. "Farewell, Mouse."

"Goodbye, Bear," murmured Mouse.

Bear closed his eyes. He lay very still.

He began to snore.

After a long while, Bear opened his eyes. He saw Mouse.

"I feel better," Bear said.

Mouse nodded, but he didn't look so good himself. His eyes were watery and he made sniffling sounds.

"Perhaps you'd better lie down," said Bear, getting out of bed.

Mouse didn't argue.

"Do you want to make a will?" Bear asked.

Mouse shook his head.

Bear carefully tucked him in. "I'm sorry you're ill," he said.

"Tank you, Bear," Mouse sniffled. And after a moment, he added,

"Dat was just the ting."

Bear smiled.

And Mouse closed his eyes and was soon fast asleep.